For
Romany, Willie, Joe,
and Harry

Copyright © 1993 by Helen Oxenbury

First U.S. edition 1994
First published in the Netherlands in 1993
by Uitgeverij J.H. Gottmer/H.J.W. Becht B.V.

Library of Congress Cataloging-in-Publication Data

Oxenbury, Helen.
It's my birthday / Helen Oxenbury.—1st U.S. ed.
Summary: The birthday child's animal friends bring ingredients
and help make a birthday cake.
ISBN 1-56402-412-1
[1. Cake—Fiction.   2. Birthdays—Fiction.   3. Animals—Fiction.]
I. Title.
PZ7.0975It   1994
[E]—dc20   93-39667

4 6 8 10 9 7 5 3

Printed in Hong Kong

The pictures in this book were done in watercolor.

Candlewick Press
2067 Massachusetts Avenue
Cambridge, Massachusetts 02140

It's My Birthday

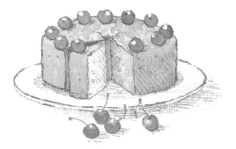

Helen Oxenbury

CANDLEWICK PRESS
CAMBRIDGE, MASSACHUSETTS

"It's my birthday and
I'm going to make a cake."

"It's my birthday and
I'm going to make a cake.
I need some eggs."

"I'll get you some eggs,"
said the chicken.

"It's my birthday and
I'm going to make a cake.
I've got the eggs.
But I need some flour."

"I'll get you some flour,"
said the bear.

"It's my birthday and
    I'm going to make a cake.
    I've got the eggs and the flour.
    But I need some butter and milk."

"I'll get you some butter and milk,"
            said the cat.

"It's my birthday and
I'm going to make a cake.
I've got eggs, flour, butter, and milk.
But I need a pinch of salt."

"I'll get you a pinch of salt,"
said the pig.

"It's my birthday and
   I'm going to make a cake.
   I've got eggs, flour, butter, milk,
   and a pinch of salt.
   But I need some sugar."

"I'll get you some sugar,"
      said the dog.

"It's my birthday and
  I'm going to make a cake.
  I've got eggs, flour, butter, milk,
  a pinch of salt, and sugar.
  But I need some
  cherries for the top."

"I'll get you some cherries for the top,"
              said the monkey.

"It's my birthday and
   I'm going to make a cake.
   I've got everything I need."

"We'll all help you make the cake,"
   said the chicken, the bear,
   the cat, the pig, the dog,
   and the monkey.

"Thank you, everybody.
   Now all of you can . . .

. . . help me eat the cake!"

"Happy Birthday!"